Dream Away

LIANA BROOKS

OTHER WORKS

ALL I WANT FOR CHRISTMAS

All I Want For Christmas Is A Reaper
All I Want For Christmas Is A Werewolf

FLEET OF MALIK

Bodies In Motion
Change of Momentum

HEROES AND VILLAINS

Even Villains Fall In Love
Even Villains Go To The Movies
Even Villains Have Interns
Even Villains Play The Hero (omnibus)
The Polar Terror

TIME AND SHADOWS
The Day Before
Convergence Point
Decoherence

SHORTER WORKS

Fey Lights
Prime Sensations
Darkness and Good

Find other works by the author at
www.lianabrooks.com

Dream Away

INKLET #52

LIANA BROOKS

Inkprint PRESS

www.inkprintpress.com

Print ISBN: 978-1-925825-54-1
eBook ISBN: 9781393418900

www.inkprintpress.com

National Library of Australia Cataloguing-in-Publication Data
Brooks, Liana 1982 –
Dream Away
50 p.
ISBN: 978-1-925825-54-1
Inkprint Press, Canberra, Australia
1. Fiction—Science Fiction—Cyberpunk 2. Fiction—Science Fiction—Crime & Mystery 3. Fiction—Fantasy—Paranormal 4. Fiction—Holidays 4. Fiction—Short Stories

First Print Edition: February 2021
Cover photo © Elvina1331 via Pixabay
Cover design © Inkprint Press
Interior art © Amy Laurens

DREAM AWAY

"Sir, how would you like to take your dream vacation today?"

The young woman smiling at Jazin as he tried to hurry down the packed commuter tunnel was a perky little thing. Cute button nose, cinnamon-colored hair, and pale-gold freckles on skin a few shades darker than her hair. She waved a synthpaper brochure at him. "Where do you want to go?"

"Home," Jazin said, avoiding eye contact. "My bank account doesn't match my dreams."

She stepped out from behind the table, her ivy-green skirt swirling as she moved. "I have dream vacations for all budgets."

"Yeah?" And he was going to get a promotion to a corner office. Just as soon as the moon turned blue. "Does this dream vacation come with paid leave?"

The young woman smiled impishly. "No leave time required. This really is a *dream* vacation." With a touch of her finger, the brochure projected a hologram of him on a white sand beach. "Do you know the average dream lasts less than five minutes? With Dream Away's new REMtech Dream 6K, you can have a week's worth of luxury in five minutes."

Jazin pushed the brochure away. "Thanks, but no thanks. I can't afford a vacation, real or otherwise."

"Oh, but you can!" she insisted. "Give me a minute, I'll give you the perfect day. Give me five minutes, and I'll give you a week in paradise. Give me an hour, and I can give you a life-time!"

He shot her a skeptical glare. "You will give me a sticky chair to nap in that stinks of other people and hasn't been sanitized in a week. Thanks, but pass."

He sidestepped and kept walking.

"Come on," she cajoled, dancing to keep up. "Would it hurt to try it?"

"Yes. I'd like to pay my rent this week, thanks all the same."

She licked her lips and glanced back at the stall. "What if I... gave you a taste? For free."

He stopped outright and looked her over. "Sounds like you're pedaling hard addictives, lady."

"Oh, no!" She shook her head and her beaded earrings jingled a soft mel-ody. "Dream Away's product is one hundred percent non-addictive."

Jazin rolled his eyes. "I bet. I nap, I walk away and the dream's forgotten in ten minutes anyway. Everybody knows dreams don't last."

"Dream Away dreams do." She placed a small, elegant hand on the crook of his arm and peered up at him, green eyes wide. "In one minute I can give you the perfect day. You want the corner office? It's yours. Want to be the star of your favorite sports team? Done. You want a day to catch up on your reading? I have all the books waiting for you. You'll feel the pages in your hands, smell the paper and ink, and when you open your eyes you'll remember the book just as if you'd spent the day reading."

He frowned. "And then I'll want another hit. Which will cost me— what—a day's wages? A week's? It's not worth it."

She shook her head determinedly. "Dream Away provides no more endorphins than you would get from a thirty minute run at the gym. And while we can't burn calories for you like a run will, we can offer you a reduction of mental stress. You won't get a real sunburn at the pool in the Jawamai Mountains. You won't really eat draris fruit in the orchards of the Old King. The new friends you meet won't be real. But you'll remember all of it like it was. It really is the perfect vacation."

"How will I remember it?" he demanded, gripping his briefcase tighter. "Are you going to dribble fruit juice on my chin?"

"Even things you experience while awake are merely secondary sensations processed by the brain. Originally created to combat depression, the REMtech Dream 6K is the delightful side outcome of Dr Wria's research into retraining brains after traumatic injury. While it initially relied on preprogrammed dreamscapes, the new

Dream Away is now sensitive enough to respond to sensations perceived by your brain, allowing you to design your own dream as you experience it."

"So you can't guarantee I won't have a nightmare." He knew there had to be a catch. There was *always* a catch.

The girl hooked her arm through his elbow and steered him toward the store. Brightly-colored travel calendars and pictures of famous buildings lined the walls. "We do exert a little control," she said reassuringly. "The REM Tech Dream 6K enhances your dream thoughts by triggering the respective neurons. You think of a fruit and by your first dream-bite, you will taste the perfect fruit. Using the same technology, we can steer dreams so that you stay in a pleasant and happy state, whatever that may be for you." She shrugged. "Or not. We don't judge."

He watched as one of the booths opened and a smiling man walked out, chatting happily with a blue-skinned woman wearing the same green skirt as the girl. The man wore a low-level maintenance worker's uniform, but instead of a laborer's perpetual frown, he looked as if he'd never had a bad day.

"A regular customer," the girl said. "He comes in every few days for a three-minute dream. Says it's like getting an extra weekend."

"And how much of his pay are you stealing?"

"Small packages have small prices," she said. "He pays two credits, only a quarter hour's wages for him. Fifteen minutes' worth of pay and he gets three days in paradise."

Jazin snorted. "And I bet he can't tell reality from fairyland anymore."

Her smile grew amused. "Dream Away does complete product testing before putting anything on the market. You'll find, as our researchers did, that it is easy to differentiate dreams from reality. You retain the memory of the place, but the human mind always knows where it is. That gentleman has been doing classes and training prep during his dream sessions. Dream Away is helping him get a better job."

The blue-skinned girl started chatting up another prospective customer in the busy transit corridor.

He sighed. That was life, wasn't it? Rush to work, hustle all day, rush to catch the next tram home. Every day was regulated down to the minute. His pay meant he had sixty minutes a week of running water, four hours a week of electricity, and a single meal box with seventeen nutritional meals a week. The other meals he either had to skip or spend money on at a company restaurant.

The girl nudged his shoulder. "One minute and I'll make all your cares go away."

"One minute?"

"The perfect day. And the first time is free."

"Fine." Jazin waved to the back of the store. "Fine. I'll try it. It's the only way you'll let me go."

"You won't be disappointed!" she bubbled. Grabbing his hand, she dragged him back to a small parlor painted entirely black. "Don't worry about the color. This is just to keep light reflection down. Please, have a seat."

A black plethasynth chair sat in the middle of the room with a green light shining out of diodes along the headrest. "That's it?"

"The REMtech Dream 6K is a very advanced machine. We don't need wires and cables everywhere to do this. After all, this is the age of nanotech!"

"All right." Reluctantly he shrugged off his coat. "Um..."

The girl pointed to the wall. "There is a locker there. You can code it to your handprint just like the lockers at work."

The ubiquitous Quaslin LockerShop lockers. Seventy years ago Quaslin had been a minor repair company and now a person couldn't turn around without seeing their logo plastered on some piece of metal. That was the advantages of having one of the only metal refineries left in operation. But at least he knew his belongings would be safe.

He tucked his briefcase and coat in, double checked the lock, and reset the code.

"You'll only be asleep for a minute," the girl soothed.

Spoken like a woman who wouldn't lose her job if the boss found out she'd been casual with a company briefcase. It didn't matter that he didn't have rank, or secrets to hide; the company was in open conflict with three other major corporations, and any sign of indiscretion meant a pink slip and your name on the station blacklist.

"Sit here, sir, and I'll adjust everything for your optimal comfort."

Jazin eyed the chair and then heaved a sigh. "Fine." He sat down and noticed wrist braces on the arms of the seat.

The girl followed his worried gaze. "Those are there for your safety. About twenty percent of our clients experience sleep-walking tendencies, involuntary and uncontrolled movement, while dreaming. The straps keep you from waking up with a black eye." She snapped the locks shut and a screen on the ceiling lit up.

The words I AM FULLY AWAKE glowed pink in the darkness.

"What's that?"

"That is the voice control panel for the restraints. When you wake up you read the words provided and the machine will release you. Would you like to try it?"

"I am fully awake," Jazin read aloud.

The word RHUBARB appeared in the same soft glow.

"Rhubarb," Jazin read obediently.

The restraints unsnapped with metallic click.

"Ready for your perfect day?" the girl asked as she locked him back in.

He settled back into the soft arms of the machine. "Sure, let's do this."

"Where would you like your perfect day to be?"

Jazin shook his head. "I don't know. The beach sounds nice. I've never been there."

"Then off to the beach it is. Sweet dreams!"

The lights dimmed and he heard the door shut. He took a deep breath, blinked, and he was standing on the beach with a hot sun beating down on his bare arms.

A white bird swooped overhead, shrieking. Just ahead, a shack of some kind looked like it was selling drinks. It seemed like a promising direction.

• • • • • • • • • •

She lifted the ident card off the corpse in the chair. Jazin Reirs, software technician, second-class. Middle-aged, overweight, single, and stupid as a box of rocks. He'd carried encrypted documents to and from work every day and never known the value. Poor fool. If he had guessed, maybe he could have sold the papers and bought some protection.

Her ear comm crackled. "How is our friend?"

"Dreaming. Permanently. I have everything we need."

"Then get out. We have another target for you."

She folded the papers and tucked them into a locked carry-case hidden in the garter on her thigh, then locked the dream parlor behind her. The nice young lady she'd rented the room from waved as she showed another prospective client the latest in TuyongTech virtual reality.

Experience the beach in real time, sand in your shoes is extra!

It was true what they said: people who spent their lives dreaming of a better future never were awake enough to make one.

THE MAKING OF
DREAM AWAY

Working from home and raising kids doesn't lend itself to vacations. Even if you go somewhere, the work and the kids tend to come with you. So I dreamed of a mini-vacation, a device that would let you escape for an hour or two...

And then things went wrong.

In retrospect, maybe we should've released this Inklet in 2020...

Read more by Liana Brooks!

EVEN VILLAINS GO TO THE MOVIES

CHAPTER ONE

Dear Mom,

New York is everything I hoped it would be. I love this school! Last semester alone the students showed a marked improvement over the previous year. And, so far, we haven't had a single senior drop out. This might be our highest graduation rate ever.

I'm really excited by all the improvements. It makes me feel like I'm actually doing something useful. I'm in control of myself, and it's wonderful.

The date with Simon was less exciting. He's... um... "Dull as a brick" might be the right term. You'd think it would be easy to find someone who could carry on an intelligent conversation in New York, especially with Internet dating. It's 2032! But, no, this hypothesis has been proven incorrect yet again.

Give my love to Daddy, Gideon, and the minions. If Maria stops by, tell her I'm worried about her. Delilah and I talked about staging an intervention. I'm not sure, but Delilah thinks Maria will calm down once the shock of losing Martin is over. It may be just a phase.

Oh, and Blessing wrote me. She's in South Africa and loving it. She sent the most hideous picture of a giant bug ever. I forwarded it to Gideon. And I told her not to bring it back no matter how much she adores its fangs.

Your loving daughter,
Angela

APRIL IN NEW YORK City. Angela could almost taste the coming summer. She'd even rolled the car windows down to take advantage of the first warm day while she drove back from lunch. Summer would be bliss: eight weeks kid-free that she planned to fill by maxing out her tourist quota and hitting every landmark in a day's drive. By the time her second year as a teacher began in August, she would know more about New York than any native-born city slicker.

Angela parked her car and rolled the windows up. The school was experiencing an unprecedented surge in academic reform, but that didn't mean she needed to tempt the alumni with an easy steal.

A police siren screamed in the distance, echoing the fear and despair radiating from the school. It felt like the first edge of trouble, a nudging headache that made her want to snarl despite her good mood—but New York was like that, the underlying anger of the citizens scraping against her nerves until she was emotionally raw.

Public School 84 was hers though. Angela had been there long enough that she'd been able to slowly shift the mood of the school from fearful resentment to an amiable interest in learning. It was probably just a schoolyard punch-up, nothing to worry over too much.

Sipping on her smoothie, Angela headed for the impressive security array that divided the outside world from the inner sanctum of PS 84. Outside there were guns, drugs, and chaos. Beyond the arch of metal that scanned for everything from weapons to lethal viruses, there were regimented schedules, dusty dead-wood copies of Shakespeare's sonnets, and young minds ready to argue over every word she said.

One of her favorite students had spent an hour debating the merits of shoelaces. You couldn't buy that kind of doublethink.

The security guard wasn't at her usual place in the main lobby, but Angela knew the drill. She swiped her ID, scanned her fingerprint, and headed for the lunchroom where there was undoubtedly a fight emerging.

As she neared the cafeteria, however, fear washed over her like the noxious smell of a skunk in the dark.

Angela tossed her unfinished smoothie in the trash and thought of pleasant things. Bluebonnets on the Texas prairie, the smell of hot apple cider on a crisp winter night, the laughter of her baby brother, the love of her parents... She took it all, wrapping it into the idea of what her school should feel like.

At first, the collective mind of the students fought back. They were scared, and fear was a familiar friend. But she pushed, and they swayed under her will. Manipulating emotions was right up there with the ability to generate polka dots on a wall in terms of usefulness; unless she wanted to turn people into mindless slaves, there was very little she could do as far as the government was concerned. Besides, brute force wasn't her style.

Influencing things was different though. *This is different,* she told herself. She turned the corner into the cafeteria and almost jumped at the sight of Travys Freeman—top student in her AP calculus class—holding a gun.

The security guard had her Taser out and was trying to talk Travys into handing over the weapon. Terror so thick it was almost a physical force rolled off Travys.

There was no way he would hand over anything to the guard. He wanted to turn it on himself. He just hadn't worked up the nerve.

Yet. Waiting would be fatal—for someone.

Angela cleared her throat and pushed on the mob. Everyone turned, even Travys. She smiled winningly. "This isn't about the quiz yesterday, is it?" she asked, weaving between the tables.

Travys made eye contact. Big mistake. Eye contact meant she had his full attention, and once she had that, he was hers.

"Travys, I asked you a question."

"It's not about the quiz, Miss Smith." The gun wavered, not quite dropping, but he wasn't sure where to aim.

Angela laid a comforting hand on the security guard's arm. "We don't need an audience do we, Travys?"

He shook his head.

"Miss Netley, why don't you get everyone to class? The bell is ringing," Angela added as the bell marking the end of lunch rang out. The crowd stayed frozen, spellbound by the same power that kept Travys from pulling the trigger. It was risky, but she refocused, encouraging everyone to hurry away. "Everyone go to class. Not you, Travys. I want a word with you."

The security guard shook herself out of her stupor. "Come on people, get to class. What are you gawking at?"

Conversation hummed to life around her and Travys sagged. The terror that had buoyed him was gone—only crushing despair remained.

Angela took a seat across the cafeteria table from him as the students and teachers filed out. Some of them tried to stay, or shout, or intervene, but she kept them all walking.

Travys peeked up at her, his brown eyes filled with tears. "I'm sorry, Miss Smith."

"Guns don't solve anything. You know that."

He was getting ready to kill himself. She could feel it. The desire to stop the pain overwhelmed him. Angela tried to bleed it off, taking some of the despair herself. It hurt.

"What happened? You can tell me, Travys." She pushed thoughts of safety towards him. He wanted to believe, but Travys had no memories of safety. When they'd first met, he was a failing student, a scrawny sixteen-year-old who flinched when anyone raised their voice. Her power allowed her to create a sanctuary in the classroom, and in that sheltered place, he'd bloomed into a brilliant student.

"Did you get a college rejection letter?" she asked. It seemed the most probable answer.

He jerked his head to the side as if he'd been slapped. "Chris came home."

She sucked in air so fast it whistled past her teeth. "I thought he was doing twenty to life?"

"He got off on a technicality."

Chris Freeman was his son's worst nightmare. He was a dealer with an anger problem who saw his only kid as a punching bag. Angela had never met the man, although she'd wanted to rearrange his brain after meeting Travys's mother, a sweet woman who was the poster child for domestic abuse.

"What's your mom doing?"

Travys's eyes dropped to the floor. "She didn't come home from work."

Which made her smarter than Angela thought. "Maybe she didn't know he was coming home."

"She knew."

And crueler than she'd guessed: she had abandoned her son to a monster. "I'm sorry."

"I'm not going home," Travys said. His thoughts turned back to the gun. Angela could feel his longing for an escape.

"Shooting yourself won't make anything better."

He startled.

"Give me the gun. We'll make other plans for tonight. You won't go back home to him."

Travys hesitated.

"Give me the gun, Travys." She seized at his mind, making him want to please her. The desire for her approval was false—Travys was too strong-minded to need outside approval—but it worked. His arm lifted slowly, like he was fighting gravity.

"You can trust me."

"Nobody move, NYPD!"

Angela jumped. She'd been too focused on Travys to feel the approach of the police. In a split-second decision, she released her hold on Travys and reached out for the minds of the police before they could ruin everything.

It was the wrong decision.

Travys screamed in pain.

His hand convulsed around the gun, pulling the trigger, and sending a bullet through the flesh of her upper arm.

Still trying to grasp the collective mind of the police, everything blurred and Angela found herself standing near the main office in the arms of a strange man in bright green spandex.

"Travys! Hold still!"

The police were moving, too focused for her to grasp; they'd stunned and cuffed Travys before she could even figure out what had happened.

She tried to brush the man aside. "Let me go." Angela released Travys's mind and focused on herself. The man in bright green held her.

"We need to get you to the doctor," the man said.

Angela realized he wasn't holding her as much as trying to hold her arm. Blood seeped between his gloved fingers. She blinked at it. The pain was secondary to the emotional savaging she'd taken from Travys's mind.

"Stay calm. An ambulance is on the

way," the man repeated. He was trying to make eye contact. She didn't cooperate with him.

"I'll be fine. I'd like to check on my students now."

"If I hadn't rushed to your rescue, you would be dead." Confusion tinged his voice, as if he was waiting for praise.

She glared at the team hustling Travys out of the school. "If the police hadn't burst in here screaming, Travys would have handed the gun over and I wouldn't have been shot." She pushed him away. "This is your fault."

"No," said a crisp, authoritative female voice. "This is your fault."

Angela turned to look at the newcomer, an older woman with salt-and-pepper hair and a grim expression, which she recognized from a picture. Katrina Bocks, de facto government employee and chief of the United Nations Council for Superhero Control.

Not a friend.

"Miss Smith, please let the EMT examine your arm, and then I have some paperwork for you to sign."

"What sort of paperwork?" She wouldn't qualify to sign with the teachers' union until she'd worked a full school year, and she doubted the school board was prepared for this kind of situation. Besides, the chances that The Company was involved with something as benign as arranging medical leave were astronomically low. She'd sooner believe in love at first sight.

Katrina gave her a bitter smile, her emotions colored by hate and anger so violent it was almost a physical aura around her. "How long have been aware of your superpowers, Miss Smith?"

Angela played innocent. "Superpowers? I'm a teacher, but that's a generous compliment. Though some days I can't imagine anything harder than twisting these young minds around calculus." She widened her eyes, the very picture of an innocent southern belle.

Katrina wasn't buying it. She held up an old-style thumb drive. "I have papers saying you are a superhero with the ability to perform psychic manipulation."

"I don't believe anyone can do that."

"I also have evidence that you and the young man were in a very unprofessional relationship. When he came to his senses and realized how he'd been used, he came to school to kill you. The public will be incensed to hear you lived." Satisfaction edged Katrina's words. She thought she had Angela pinned in a corner.

The woman had come far too well-prepared.

Angela looked over at the EMT hovering behind them. Time for a quick getaway. "I think I need to see the doctor now."

"I'll wait with you," the man offered. "For your protection."

Right, he was her well-meaning bodyguard, another concerned citizen fighting for truth, justice, and the American way. Angela moved to walk past Katrina, then stopped. "How long have you been tracking me?"

"I learned several months ago that a mind-raper was in the area. I didn't know who it was until today."

Angela nodded. Considering they didn't know the name of their target, they had certainly put a plan together quickly. Daddy was not going to like hearing about this. There was always a risk of The Company stumbling across her path this close to headquarters, but things had been so quiet lately she'd been sure she was flying under the radar. "I'll meet you at the hospital, I suppose?"

Katrina smiled triumphantly. "Yes. There's some very simple paperwork you need to fill out. And then we'll discuss more of your future after your surgery."

Her arm stung at the reminder. "I don't think I need surgery, just stitches."

"And I don't think a mutant should be allowed to breed," Katrina said. "Fortunately, the government sees my point of view. A quick snip-snip and you'll be safe to release into the wild."

Angela turned to follow the EMT, teeth clenched hard enough to hurt. There were so many things she wanted to say. None of them would help. Training took over, memories of summer drills under the hot Texas sun. The Company could come at any time. There was no hope of fighting them, so you had to evade, dodge, run.

She let the EMT load her into the back of the ambulance and waited until they'd hit the first stoplight before she dialed the only number that mattered. "Mom, they found me. Come pick me up."

Keep reading! Head to
<u>www.inkprintpress.com/lianabrooks/</u>
<u>heroesandvillains/movies/</u>
to buy your copy now!

ABOUT THE AUTHOR

Liana Brooks is a fulltime novelist and mom who would dearly love a vacation. She enjoys writing science fiction in every form, from sprawling space operas romances (the *Fleet of Malik* series, starting with *Bodies In Motion*), to the antics of a super-powered family (the *Heroes and Villains* series, which can be read in any order), to intricate time-travel murder mysteries (the *Time And Shadow* series, starting with *The Day Before*).

Liana also maintains a soft spot for paranormal romances. She writes the popular *All I Want For Christmas* novellas, including *All I Want For Christmas Is A Werewolf* and *All I Want For Christmas Is A Reaper*.

You can learn more about her and her books at www.LianaBrooks.com

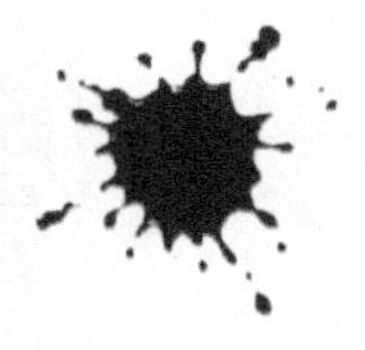

INKLETS

Collect them all! Released on the 1st and 15th of each month.

INKLET #055
Allure
AMY LAURENS

INKLET #056
The LIES We KNOW
LIANA BROOKS

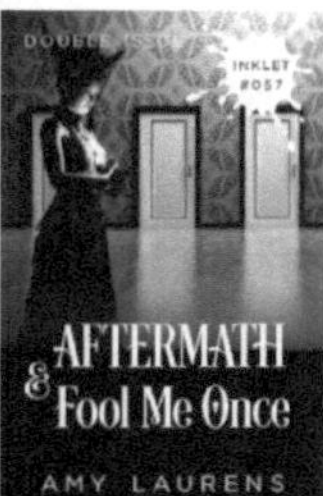

DOUBLE
INKLET #057
AFTERMATH
& Fool Me Once
AMY LAURENS

INKLET #058
Purity
An Age Of Unicorns Story
AMY LAURENS

INKLET #059
Saved
AMY LAURENS

INKLET #060
A Kiss is the Secret
AMY LAURENS

INKLET #061
A Changing Tides Story
Fire Bright
AMY LAURENS

INKLET #062
Hades AND Persephone
LIANA BROOKS

INKLET #063
Just So Long As You're Happy
AMY LAURENS

INKLET #064
Theft Of A Lifetime
LIANA BROOKS

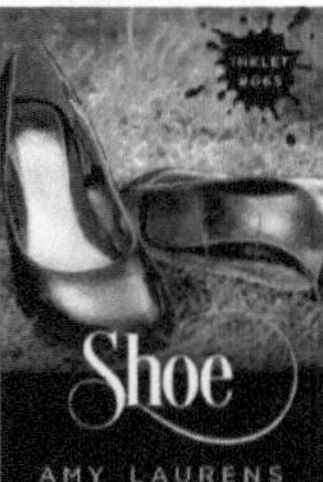
INKLET #065
Shoe
AMY LAURENS

INKLET #066
Published AUTHOR
LIANA BROOKS

DOUBLE ISSUE
INKLET #067
THE REMARKABLE INSIGHT OF JELLYBEANS & Understanding
AMY LAURENS

INKLET #068
Desperate Measures
AMY LAURENS

INKLET #069
Rock-a-bye
LIANA BROOKS

INKLET #070
the Other Carly
AMY LAURENS

INKLET #071
Bs By Bioluminescent Light
AMY LAURENS

INKLET #072
Even Villains Grant Wishes
A Heroes & Villains Story
LIANA BROOKS

www.ingramcontent.com/pod-product-compliance
Lightning Source LLC
Chambersburg PA
CBHW032052180726

48284CB00004B/1309